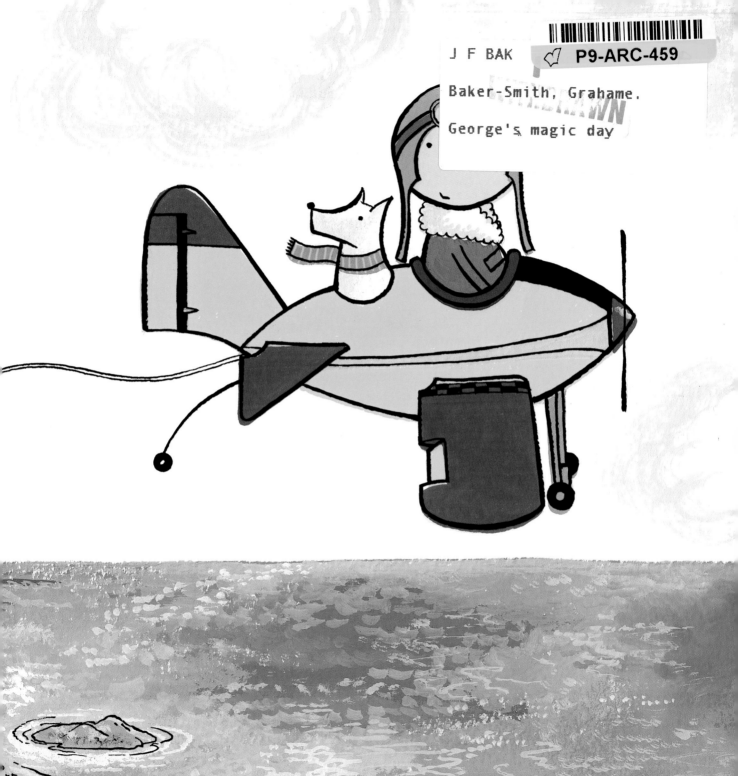

To Lillie, who seemed to bring these characters with her.

LITTLE PILOT: George's Magic Day
by Grahame Baker Smith

British Library Cataloguing in Publication Data
A catalogue record of this book is available from
the British Library.

ISBN 0340 87549 6 (HB)   0340 87550 X (PB)
Little Pilot: George's Magic Day © 2005 Grahame Baker Smith.

The right of Grahame Baker Smith to be identified
as the author and the illustrator of this Work
has been asserted by him in accordance with
the Copyright, Designs and Patents Act 1988.

First published 2005
2 4 6 8 10 9 7 5 3 1

Published by Hodder Children's Books,
a division of Hodder Headline Limited,
338 Euston Road, London, NW1 3BH

Printed in China

A **Little Pilot** Adventure

George's Magic Day

Grahame Baker Smith

Hodder Children's Books

A division of Hodder Headline Limited

George had always wanted
to fly. From the top of the
Great Tree, the jungle
stretched forever.

'Oh if only I had wings,'
said George.

Swinging fast was exciting...

But it wasn't flying!

George sat down to think.
All he needed were
some feathers.

One, two, three...
wheee!

'I'm flying,'
cried George.

But he wasn't...

CRASH!

Luckily
his friends
were there
to catch him.

'Cheer up George,'
they said.

Hula Hula Hippo
danced for him.

Pablo the Lion painted a wonderful picture.

And Love Leopard gave him a HUGE hug.

But nothing seemed to work...

George was still sad and off he went
deep into the jungle.

His friends didn't know
how to help him.
When...

Brrrrrrrrrrrrrrmmmm

mmmmmmm.

'Look out,'
    yelled Hula Hula.
        'What's up?' roared Pablo.
            'Who's that?' called Love Leopard.

It was Little Pilot and Flyboy!

Love Leopard spoke first.

'Can you find our friend, George?'
he asked.

'Of course,' said Little Pilot.
He climbed back into the
big flying thing and

OOOOOOOOOOOOooooMMMMMMM.

He soon spotted George swinging sadly
by the edge of the swamp. And there was
Snappodile sneaking towards him...

'Hello little monkey,' said Snappodile.
'Why so sad?'
'I want to fly,' said George gloomily,
'but I don't think monkeys are meant to.'
'Oh I don't know,' said Snappodile.
'Climb on my tail and I'll show you how.'

With a smile on his face
and a flick of his tail,
Snappodile launched
George high into
the sky...

...just as Little Pilot appeared.

George was flying at last!

Three cheers for Little Pilot.

'Hip, hip, hooray,' they shouted once.

'Hip, hip, hooray,' they shouted twice.

And George's voice was the loudest of all...

Hip, hip, Hoooraaaaay!

Until next time,

GOODBYE!